TABLE OF CONTENTS

You see, it happens to me often. I formulate my ideas, prayers, unconventional. They happen to me; I don't ask for myself, for my children, I have been 16 times to Medjugorje, each time I return with the will to return soon, immediately.

I have been going there since 2007, two or three times a year. I have seen the "signs" that many, not all of them see, the sun beating, turning, turning red and yellow, moving to the sides, etc...

I feel the scent of roses, even during the ascent to Podrobo, the mountain of apparitions, I dare to speak with my heavenly mother, it is a prayer, in my way, but sincere with absolute faith ... later I realize that I am the answer is given, in grace, never for me, I don't ask for me, I'm ashamed ...

The first time I went, I stayed five days, and I had the tears of joy, which flowed without realizing it, dried them, but continued.

Mass, the ascent to Mount Podrobo and Krizwak, was a joy, even barefoot, on the sharp stones, without hurting me. Still, I had joy in my heart. I was in the home of the HEAVENLY MOTHER, I felt her presence continuously, I had peace inside, and the same thought, "I have to go back."

I brought Sergio, Luigi, Bruno, and the grace of joy touched all; the mass in the Church of San Giacomo was a hint of peace, serenity, confession, communion, even kneeling on the ground, the Church was always full...

Then the first signal came, direct, assertive, disruptive, one November night, I was sleeping, tired from the journey, and suddenly at about midnight, I wake up suffocated, smelling of pink, very sweet, but it was the only mine, in the room was my wife, who does not hear anything

I wandered around the room, bathroom, open the door, window, the perfume was suffocating, it didn't go away, I thought a bottle of perfume had fallen in the bathroom, it wasn't that ... hard about 10 minutes, I didn't check the clock, and all of a sudden he ended ... I sat in bed, with thoughts overwhelming me from each other, and why? To me? Questions that had no answers ... it was not a dream, I got up, walked, opened the window, it was freezing and foggy, it wasn't time for roses ... after I don't know how long I went back to sleep, the tiredness of the bus trip had its place...

But the night was not over, everything was repeated in the morning, maybe at 4, I woke up again on the skid, scared, what happens, but why? No answer. Did you go on for more or less the same time, without interruptions, intense, penetrating; I was out of breath, for fear? Amazement? I didn't give logical explanations, and I didn't...

The next day I spoke to the priest who accompanied us, he told ME, the HEAVENLY MOTHER wanted to give you a personal welcome, she is close to you, do not worry ... (Friar Raffaele, was one of the servants of Mary, of the Basilica of Monte Berico in Vicenza) that I knew well by now, we had already made many pilgrimages together, I was always close to him, in the bus, at the table, he was elderly, I supported him ... he had been Director in Rome of the Catholic

University, a well of science, on trips he was often at the microphone, he talked to us about everything, he was highly educated, and even sick with cancer.

Then my pilgrimages continued, many, until 2013, when I went to Medugorje with Bruno, with my car, in July, it was boiling, Medujorie is resting in a valley, surrounded by mountains, or it's so cold or so hot, even up to 35 degrees.

I went to the same pension Fontana, where we went by bus, Bruno and I had to go to a client, and I thought of stopping (I would never come back without stopping).

We paused at the boarding house with dear Cornelia, the owner, who welcomed us with her mother's smile.

All her family runs the Pension Fontana, she, her husband, and three children. She is a lady who helped in the kitchen, she was generous in portions, the wine and grappa she made, the happiness she transmitted to us was contagious, even if you were tired as soon as you arrived (it's 900 km) you felt at home.

In the afternoon we decided to rest Bruno and me, with the agreement to wake up before 16.00 to go to the confessionals, which started at 16.00, I was happy to be in Medugorje. It was now my home ... I knew the shopkeepers on the street, I greeted, smiled; I had arrived in the best place you wanted.

I said to Bruno, I'll put the alarm in my cell phone and wake you up ... and so I did

Everyone in his room we have fallen into restful sleep ... the alarm clock rang; I picked up my mobile phone, turned it off and held it in my hand against my chest. Without realizing I went back to sleep ... I don't know how long it passed. Still, I was awakened by a jolt of the bed, in the hips and from head to toe, it was not a tremor, it was a dance, of course, I was about to go down, but I fell to the ground, and ran towards the exit of the pension, thinking about the earthquake ...

When I got to the exit, there was the Cornelia, who, seeing me frightened, stopped me, telling Giuseppe where you go in your underwear, undershirt, and barefoot.

I shouted, the earthquake, earthquake, meanwhile the brain was wondering? But there is no earthquake? ... Then it was a shock I said to myself?

it was no shake or earthquake ... then I went back to my room, thinking I had dreamed? (To give me an excuse) I called Bruno in the other room, which was regularly snoring, and asked, did you feel the earthquake? He immediately replied no, and it wasn't the earthquake, she was still my HEAVENLY MOTHER, she was worried that I would go to confessionals quickly.... everyone knows that it takes hours to queue to confess.

After the confessionals were occupied by rows of people, mostly Italians, where there were Italian priests, I saw a French priest with three in front of me. I waited and entered.

Immediately my word fell on the subject of the fact that happened a little earlier,

That was what I wanted to understand, knowing that he could never give me logical explanations

I was excited and stammering, I used French, but slowly I explained, the father smiled, he was happy, took my hands in his ... and said, did you arrive today? YES I said, Our Lady gave you a welcome greeting, you are in her heart, here in Medujorie these things happen, not to everyone, by signals, she loves this land, the pilgrims, and she knows how to read in your sincere heart, she loves you...

I said, but Father, why me? And what should I do?

He advised me, do apostolate, talks about this experience of yours, do not be ashamed, and not even be presumptuous, tries to be humble.

He gave me the solution, and I went out, but I had to sit on the outside benches. I was happy, delighted, my legs were shaking with emotion ... I mean, my faith has strengthened, I had no doubts, but now this is a kind of a prize? Jesus, I thought, forgive me, did I disturb you? And your kind maternal MOM has rewarded me? But I don't want to be rewarded, sir, I commit many sins ... I am not a perfect Christian!

Since then, the MATERNAL NOSTALGIA was born in my heart, and I think if you want me, I'm here, take care of it...

The Blessed Virgin Mary has told the visionaries of Medjugorje that she would impart to them Ten Secrets. Very little is known about these secrets, though we know that some of them have to do with chastisements for the world. We also know that the third secret will be a visible, lasting sign that will miraculously be placed somewhere on Apparition Hill. It will be permanent, indestructible, and beautiful. Also, both Mirjana and Vicka have stated that part of the seventh secret no longer exists because of the prayers and fasting of the people responding to Our Lady's call.

The six Medjugorje visionaries in the beginning day of the apparitions. Our Lady has entrusted secrets to them that will once be revealed bring about sweeping conversions throughout the world. Three of the visionaries have all Ten Secrets, while the other three have nine. From left to right, as of June 25, 2009 – Ivan has nine secrets; Marija has nine secrets; Ivanka has ten secrets; Mirjana has ten secrets; Jakov has ten secrets, and Vicka has nine secrets.

Three of the visionaries, Mirjana, Ivanka, and Jakov, have all ten secrets and no longer see Our Lady daily. Mirjana received the 10th secret in 1982, Ivanka in 1985, and Jakov in 1998. The other three visionaries, Ivan, Marija, and Vicka, each have nine secrets and still see Our Lady daily, as of June 1, 2009.

Mirjana was the first visionary to receive all ten secrets. Our Lady has given her the responsibility of revealing the secrets. Mirjana knows the day and date of each of the secrets. Our Lady told Mirjana to choose a priest to reveal the secrets to the world. Mirjana chose **Father Petar Ljubicic**. Ten days before the first secret is revealed, Father Petar will be given a parchment containing the Ten Secrets. When Father Petar receives the parchment, he will only be able to read the first secret. During the ten days, Father Petar, along with Mirjana, spends the first seven days in fasting and prayer. Three days before the event takes place, he is to announce it to the world. At the proper time, he will be able to see and read the second secret, then the third, etc., according to Heaven's schedule. Mirjana said that Father Petar doesn't have the right to choose whether to say or not to say them. He accepted this mission, and he has to fulfill that according to God's Will.

**MIRJANA HAS RELAYED
THE FOLLOWING**

"Before the visible sign is given to humankind, there will be three warnings to the world. The warnings will be in the form of events on earth. Mirjana will be a witness to them. Ten days before one of the warnings, Mirjana will notify a priest of her choice. As stated earlier, Fr. Petar was the priest she chose. The witness of Mirjana will be a confirmation of the apparitions and a stimulus for the conversion of the world.

"After the warnings, the visible sign will appear on the site of the apparitions in Medjugorje for all the people to see. The sign will be given as a testimony, confirming the apparitions and calling people back to faith.

"The ninth and tenth secrets are profound. They concern chastisement for the sins of the world. Punishment is inevitable, for we cannot expect the whole world to be converted. The punishment can be diminished by prayer and penance, but it cannot be eliminated. Mirjana says that one of the evils that threatened the world, the one contained in the seventh secret, has been averted thanks to prayer and fasting. That is why the Blessed Virgin continues to encourage prayer and fasting:

'You have forgotten that through prayer and fasting, you can avert wars and suspend the laws of nature.'

"After the first warning, the others will follow in a relatively short time. Thus, people will have some time for conversion.
"That interval will be a period of grace and conversion. After the visible sign appears, those who are still alive will have little time for conversion. For that reason, the Blessed Virgin invites us to urgent conversion and reconciliation. The invitation to prayer and penance is meant to avert evil and war, but most of all, to save souls.

"According to Mirjana, the events predicted by the Blessed Virgin are near. Under this experience, Mirjana proclaims to the world: 'Convert as quickly as possible.

"In addition to this basic message, Mirjana related an apparition she had in 1982, which we believe sheds some light on some aspects of Church history. She spoke of an apparition in which Satan appeared to her. Satan asked Mirjana to renounce the Madonna and follow him. That way, she could be happy in love and life. He said that following the Virgin, on the contrary, would only lead to suffering. Mirjana rejected him, and immediately the Virgin gave her the following message, in a substance:

'Excuse me for this, but you must realize that Satan exists. One day he appeared before the throne of God and asked permission to submit the Church to a period of trial. God permitted him to try the Church for one century. This century is under the power of the devil, but when the secrets confided to you come to pass, his power will be destroyed.

Even now, he is beginning to lose his power and has become aggressive. He is destroying marriages, creating division among priests, and is responsible for obsessions and murder. You must protect yourselves against these things through fasting and prayer, especially community prayer. Carry sacred objects with you. Put them in your house, and restore the use of holy water.'"

Even though Our Lady doesn't speak a lot about the secrets, they are an essential part of Our Lady's plans for humankind's salvation. For those responding to Our Lady's call, the secrets should not create fear in their hearts. Any good father disciplines his children. The secrets are God's way of disciplining His wayward children back into His loving embrace. The secrets will be fearful and considered chastisements for those of His children who have turned away from Him, who are living godless lives. But Our Lady calls all of us to conversion, not to wait until the secrets are realized. For many, it will then be too late. Act now and embrace Our Lady's messages. Accept and embrace God's love and mercy during this particular time of grace with Our Lady.

I acknowledge that personal factors may have well caused the teenagers' initial encounters with the Virgin. For example, Ivanka, who was the first to perceive a visitation, had just lost her natural mother. The perception of apparitional experiences spread rapidly among her intimate peer group. ...The region's tension and anxiety likely exacerbated this contagion process and the need to believe among the youthful protagonists.

Skeptical investigator Joe Nickell has noted several reasons for doubting the authenticity of the apparitions, such as contradictions in the stories. For example, on the first sighting, the teenagers claimed they had visited Podrida Hill to smoke. They later retracted this, claiming they had gone to the hill to pick flowers. According to

Nickell, there is also a problem with the "embarrassingly illiterate" nature of the messages.

The messages given by Our Lady in Medjugorje began on June 25, 1981, and continue to this day. The earliest messages from 1981-1983, recorded by the parish in Medjugorje (Information Center MIR Medjugorje, were unfortunately confiscated and destroyed by the communists.

The 1981-1983 messages found here were obtained from Fr. René Laurentin and Professor René LeJeune. They were initially recorded in French and translated into English by Juan Gonzales Jr., Ph.D. Although the parish has not validated these messages in Medjugorje, great care was taken to record, translate, and compile.

We have also included messages compiled by Fr. Laurentin and Prof. LeJeune from 1984-1986, which are in addition to the weekly messages recorded by the parish in Medjugorje during that same period.

"Dear children! I am calling you to prayer, fasting, and renunciation at this time that

you may be stronger in faith. This is a time of awakening and of giving birth. As nature which gives itself, you also, little children, ponder how much you have received. Be joyful bearers of peace and love that it may be good for you on earth. Yearn for Heaven, and in Heaven, there is no sorrow or hatred. That is why, little children, decide anew for conversion and let holiness begin to reign in your life. Thank you for having responded to my call."

Miracle at Medjugorje: A Transpersonal Interpretation It is impossible to give a complete account of the events tied to the apparitions and messages from the Blessed Virgin Mary (BVM) that have issued from the remote mountain village of Medjugorje (pronounced meh'-jobe-goo-yeh) in the former Yugoslavia since 1981 and continue to this day. I can only refer the psychologist interested in religious issues to the abundant literature about the phenomenon in printed materials and on the Internet (see, for example, Davies, 2004; Gramaglia, 1987; Jones, 1994; Laurentin, 1987; Sivric, 1989). According to Google, the number of references about "Medjugorje" on the Internet is quite large. There is little indication that public interest in the apparitions of Medjugorje is dying down. The disinterested observer will find that most Internet references are widely enthusiastic, almost fanatically credulous, and evangelical in their description of the phenomenon.

Official documents and declarations of the Roman Catholic Church are much more reserved in their judgment and, in fact, assert that it is impossible to prove or affirm that the Madonna has ever appeared to anyone in Medjugorje (Davies, 2004). For the sake of argument, I will assume that the apparitions at Medjugorje are genuine and conclude with a brief discussion of what it would mean if the apparitions were not authentic.

Faithful and Not True In absolute terms, the apparitions of Medjugorje are accurate and not actual. As representations of unconscious knowledge, they are right; as representations of physical reality, they are false, in the same way, that a map is not the territory, the menu is not the meal, the sign is not the destination, and the written or spoken word is not the thought or feeling it intends to convey or express. Symbols are not to be taken literally or mistaken for the reality they represent. People encounter difficulty when they mistake the symbol for reality during their encounter with the inner order events. When we do mistake the symbolic appearance for the reality itself, we inevitably misunderstand its nature. This is not to say that there is no reality behind the symbols. As Jung correctly understood, the world of imagination and so-called symbols and myths are in many ways more real or closer to the way reality is than what is often referred to as physical, material, "sensory-hard" facts or phenomenon we can see, hear, feel smell, and touch (Jung, 1960). Dreams, ideas, emotions, values, and other aspects of psychological life are as real and, in some instances, more real than the chair upon which we sit because of their effect upon our experience of ourselves and our world. Television characters of a favorite TV program, for example, may attain a level of reality that is more real, more tangible, and more substantial than the lives of the actual actors who portray those characters in the mind of its viewers. Imaginative constructs, such as Darwin's theory of evolution, Freud's speculation about the nature of personality, Existentialism's philosophy about the nature of existence, and science's "Big Bang" conjecture about the origin of the universe have structured generations of people's experience of themselves and their world. Nor is it sufficiently appreciated how waking experience is directed, cultures and civilizations are formed, and religious and political structures are maintained by using our imaginative abilities.

MIRACLE AT
MEDJUGORJE

A TRANSPERSONAL INTERPRETATION

It is impossible to give a complete account of the events tied to the apparitions and messages from the Blessed Virgin Mary (BVM) issued from the remote mountain village of Medjugorje (pronounced *meh'-job-got-yeh*) in the former Yugoslavia since 1981 and continue to this day. I can only refer the psychologist interested in religious issues to the abundant literature about the phenomenon in printed materials and on the Internet (see, for example, Davies, 2004; Gramaglia, 1987; Jones, 1994; Laurentin, 1987; Sivric, 1989). According to Google, the number of references about "Medjugorje" on the Internet is quite large. There is little indication that public interest in the apparitions of Medjugorje is dying down. The disinterested observer will find that most Internet references are widely enthusiastic, almost fanatically credulous, and evangelical in their description of the phenomenon). Official documents and declarations of the Roman Catholic Church are much more reserved in their judgment and, in fact, assert that it is impossible to prove or affirm that the Madonna has ever appeared to anyone in Medjugorje (Davies, 2004). For the sake of argument, I will assume that the apparitions at Medjugorje are genuine and conclude with a brief discussion of what it would mean if the apparitions were not authentic.

THE PHENOMENON

This particular religious phenomenon began on June 24, 1981, at the small Catholic parish of Medjugorje (with about 4,000 people) in the Republic of Bosnia- Herzegovina of the former Yugoslavia. It was on that day, a little over 27 years ago, that six Croatian adolescents, between the ages of 10 and 17 -- Vicka Ivankovic (age 17), Mirjana Dragicevic (age 16), Marija Pavlovic (age 16), Ivan Dragicevic (age 16), Ivanka Ivankovic (age 15), and Jakov Colo (age 10) -- first reported that they had seen and spoken with an apparition of the Blessed Virgin Mary (or *Gospa*, as the local Croatian Catholics call her) (First Days, 2006). The phenomenon is referred to as an "apparition" instead of a "vision" because, in a vision, there is nothing necessarily external to the percipient being perceived through the physical senses. In contrast, in an apparition, there is something external to which the percipients respond, which is what the six youths at Medjugorje claim to perceive (Laurentin, 1987, chapter 5). During the first year, the apparition appeared and spoke to the six percipients (or "Seers" as they are called in the popular literature) every day at 6:40 p.m. when they were together at a hill called Podbrdo on Mount Crnica in Medjugorje.

Today, the apparitions are no longer tied to the collective assembly of the six percipients or a particular location but to the individual percipients themselves. The percipients (all of whom are currently married) can experience the apparition separately and alone, regardless of location. Whether in Boston or Alabama, Sarajevo or Medjugorje, Italy or Switzerland, in private homes or public churches, fields or vineyards, cars or buses -- the Madonna appears and speaks for 5, 10, or 15 minutes to a percipient, while remaining invisible and inaudible to everybody else, confiding daily "messages" or particular monthly messages on the 25th of each month that are then translated and distributed to the public. The Messages' content encourages people to pray daily, especially the Rosary; fast weekly, especially on Wednesday and Fridays; read the Bible every day; confess one's sins every month; receive Holy Communion. Nine or ten different "Secrets" have also been privately conveyed to each of the percipients intended for particular groups of people (e.g., the sick, the young, priests, souls in purgatory, families).

The frequency of apparitions varies with the number of Secrets each percipient has received.

16

The Madonna appears daily to the three percipients who have received only nine Secrets (Vicka Ivankovic, Marija Pavlovic, and Ivan Dragicevic). She appears once a year to the three percipients who have received all ten Secrets -- on Christmas Day to one recipient (Jakov Colo), on the anniversary of the apparitions to another (Ivanka Ivankovic), and the birthday of a third (Mirjana Dragicevic). Only one of the Secrets has been revealed to the general public --

The miraculous appearance of a great shrine in Medjugorje in honor of Mary as a "great sign" to atheists that the apparitions are real -- an event not yet materialized, though still anticipated (Franken, 1999). All ten Secrets are expected to be revealed sometime during the lifetime of the six percipients. When all ten Secrets have been revealed to the six percipients, the apparitions will cease, and three "warnings" will occur in some manner intended to encourage the species to repent and convert to the teachings of Jesus (although necessarily to the Roman Catholic Church) and to turn away from a life of sin and the ways of Satan. The apparitions themselves were initially predicted to last for only a few days. They have continued for over 27 years -- about 60,000 times (i.e., 27 yrs. times 365 days time's six percipients) -- and theoretically could go on forever. Three of the six percipients have said the BVM had promised them apparitions for life. The second generation of percipients has emerged who hear but do not see the BVM (Jelena Vasilg and Marijana Vasilj, who live in Medjugorje).

A virtual cottage industry has grown up around the events tied to Medjugorje, including pilgrim guides and tourist agencies, merchandise and souvenirs, web sites and newsletters, brochures and prayer books, and even a Hollywood movie (*Gospa* in 1995 starring Martin Sheen and Morgan Fairchild) aimed at promoting the authenticity of the apparitions. The "Miracle of Medjugorje" has attracted an estimated 22 million pilgrims to the locale who arguably seek the apparitions to confirm their faith (Davies, 2004).

"FRUIT" OF MEDJUGORJE -

- the converted lives, the increase in piety and devotions, the recovery of lost faith --
that defenders of the apparitions point to as the ultimate sign of its authenticity. The
Congregation for the Doctrine of the Faith (CDF), the official arm of the Holy See in
Rome, while not denying the deepening of spiritual life that *has* occurred in pilgrims,
disagrees that the apparitions are its cause, and in 1991 forbid all public pilgrimages to
Medjugorje that presume it to be a place of authentic Marian apparitions ("Official
pilgrimages to Medjugorje, taken to be a place of authentic Marian apparitions, may
not be organized whether at a parish or diocesan level" (quoted in Davies, 2004, p.
169).

THE ROMAN CATHOLIC CHURCH'S POSITION

Church authorities began to question the authenticity of the Marian messages when
both the parish priest (Fr. Jozo Zovko) and local bishop (Msgr. Pavao Zanic) came to
believe that the Messages purportedly being communicated by the BVM contained
contradictions and falsehoods and reflected a specific human manipulation in the
interference of Church affairs that were deemed inappropriate for an authentic Marian
apparition (Jones, 1994; Sivric, 1989). There was the issue about Madonna's veiled
threats pressuring the local bishop to accept the apparitions ("Tell the bishop that I
seek a quick conversion from him towards the happenings in Medjugorje before it is
too late I am sending my second-last warning. If what I seek does not come about, my
judgment and the judgment of my Son awaits the bishop," quoted in Davies, 2004, p.
56). There were pastoral issues related to the Madonna's repeated defense of a priest
who had been expelled from the Franciscan Order and dispensed from his vows on the
instructions of Pope John Paul II for disobedience to superiors and for having sexual
relations with a Franciscan nun ("He is not guilty [Our Lady repeated this three times].
The bishop does not keep order. That is why he is responsible. The justice whom you
have not seen will come back," quoted in Davies, 2004, pp. 31-32).

There were commercial issues related to the Madonna promoting the sale of books favorable to the phenomenon ("Let the priests read Laurentin's book and propagate it," quoted in Davies, 2004, p. 109). There were political issues related to the Madonna taking sides on questions of parish jurisdiction -- what has been called the "Herzegovina Question" (i.e., disobedient Franciscans refusing to turn over religious parishes to diocesan clergy, establishing parishes outside the diocesan structure, erecting ecclesial buildings and forming religious communities without permission, performing invalid marriages and confirmations). Proponents of Medjugorje claim that the apparitions and the Herzegovina Question are separate issues. Bishops see them as inextricably linked with the BVM being used to justify continued Franciscan disobedience to Church authority.

Between 1981 and 1991, three ecclesiastical commissions consisting of 30 priests and physicians and 20 bishops investigated the phenomena of Medjugorje. The official conclusion of the Roman Catholic Church after ten years of investigation is expressed in the Zadar Declaration (April 9-11, 1991), which states: "Based on studies conducted so far, it cannot be affirmed that supernatural apparitions and revelations are occurring" (quoted in Davies, 2004, p. 89). In 1991, a five-year war broke out between the Republic of Croatia and Bosnia's Republic- Herzegovina. All ecclesial investigations were called to a halt, and no further official investigations by the Church into the Medjugorje apparitions have taken place since that time.

The rigor with which the Catholic Church investigates alleged "miracles" and "apparitions" is well known. Of the 6,000 claims of miraculous cures that the International Medical Committee of Lourdes has evaluated, Frances, for instance, only 64 have been identified as medically inexplicable and officially recognized as miracles by the Roman Catholic Church (Dowling, 1984). Of the 98 claims of Marian apparitions between 1347-2008 listed on The Apparitions of Jesus and Mary. Five have been disapproved by the Catholic Church (e.g., Caserta, Italy in 1916; Necedah, Wisconsin 1950- 1975; Bayside, New York in 1970s, Naju, Korea in 1985), and 24 have been recognized as authentic (e.g., Guadalupe, Mexico in 1531; Rue du Bac, France in 1830; LaSalette, France in 1846, Knock, Ireland in 1879, Beauraing, Belgium in 1932, Zietum,

Egypt in 1968; Akita, Japan in 1973; Culpa, Nicaragua in 1980). This "full Church-approved" list includes two of the most famous: Lourdes, France, wherein 1858 the BVM appeared 18 times to 14-year-old Bernadette Soubirous with the Church declaring the apparitions authentic four years later in 1862 (with no "Secrets"), and Fatima, Portugal wherein 1917 the BVM appeared six times to 10-year-old Lucia Dos Santos, 9-year-old Francisca Marto, and 7-year-old Jacinta Marto with the Church accepting the apparitions as authentic 13 years later in 1930 (with one "Secret" in three parts) (Foley, 2002). Medjugorje has not followed the same pattern as earlier, approved apparitions, and falls into the category of Marian apparitions to which Church authorities will neither approve

Nor disapprove. There has developed a palpable tension between believers in the Medjugorje apparitions who consider them genuine and ecclesiastical authorities who do not.

IS IT REAL? IS IT TRUE? IS IT GOOD?

As psychologists interested in religious issues, the questions before us are these:

- Is something "supernatural" and "miraculous" happening at Medjugorje, or do we see what could be "one of the most subversive hoaxes in the history of the Catholic Church (S. Caldwell, quoted in Davies, 2004, p. 175)?
- Are the apparitions and messages of Medjugorje solely the product of the subjective experience of the six percipients who experience them, or do they refer to some actual metaphysical reality that is producing them?
- Can a science of psychology verify the authenticity of this or any other phenomenon labeled "miraculous" and "supernatural," or is it entirely beyond the reach of psychology's existing theories and concepts, linguistic frameworks and philosophical assumptions, subject matter, and methods of inquiry?
- Can the transcendent reality to which the apparitions and messages of Medjugorje refer *ever* be addressed by the proper psychological study, or is

20

psychological science incapable of revealing the objective existence of actual transcendental realities? For that matter, can transcendent realities ever be an "object" of scientific research?

We cannot understand what the Medjugorje phenomenon is or begin answering any of these questions unless we understand the nature of personality and consciousness's characteristics.

AN EPISTEMOLOGICAL DILEMMA

The nature of the apparitions occurring at Medjugorje is so uncertain - appearing to be either miraculous and supernatural on the one hand, or conventional and unremarkable on the other, because we try to examine them from the perspective of ordinary waking consciousness and the interpretive filters of conventional religious concepts and in rational true-and-false terms. We naturally interpret the apparitions' manifestation and any symbolic meaning they may have in light of our beliefs of good and evil, the possible and the impossible, what is expected and abnormal, real and unreal. However, relying solely upon traditional religious concepts and rational accurate- or-false approaches can interpret such highly creative and essential phenomena like Medjugorje extremely difficult.

As children of our culture and the modern scientific age, we search for certainties and are taught from childhood to consider physical facts as the only criteria of reality. What is imaginary is not real. We refuse to admit into existence as "real" anything that we cannot see, hear, smell, taste, or touch through the physical senses. We don't trust anything that occurs, such as Medjugorje's apparitions, unless we have personal experience of it, are consciously aware of what is happening, how it occurs, and why. We want to know where the apparitions are coming from if they are part of the percipients' subconscious, and we want our answers given to us in a manner that our comprehending ego can understand. Our reasoning mind wants its truths labeled and clothed in clear-cut black-and-white, true-or-false terms. We seem to think that if we can name and label the apparitions of Medjugorje a "supernatural, miraculous event" on the one hand, or a "subconscious fraud" on the other, then it will be more acceptable and real.

Now it is essential to recognize, psychologically speaking, that when people pray, have authentic mystical experiences, ingest entheogens, or even use the Ouija board, they are working through areas of the psyche (Grof, 1985; Hastings, 1991; Klimo, 1987; Myers, 1976; J. Roberts, 1975; T. Roberts, 2001). At some indescribable point, the psyche opens up into levels

Reality, experience, or understanding are usually unavailable to ego-directed awareness and may personify itself to get its message across, dramatizing itself through the creativity of the percipient's beliefs and personality. Because most people do not understand their inner reality or have been taught to mistrust themselves, revelatory material must then erupt *as if* it came from an outside source if it is to be accepted or even perceived at all. Often this presents the percipient with an irreconcilable dilemma where he or she must prove that the outside source exists as it is physically perceived and interpreted -- the Blessed Virgin Mary in the case of the "apparitions" at Medjugorje -- or else lose faith in the actuality of the phenomenon, and face the fact that our perception and understanding is not infallible.

However, it is possible, and much more efficient and practical, to accept this fact and realize and acknowledge more to reality than what the physical senses can show. Much exists in that subliminal psychic realm to which we will not admit. Physics has taught me that there are many probable systems of reality and that if we consistently admit into evidence only those things we can see, hear, smell, taste, or touch, in so doing, we only appreciate half or maybe a third of reality. Mystic and writer Seth-Jane Roberts reminds us that:

As an individual's physical life rises from hidden dimensions beyond those readily accessible in physical terms. It draws its energy and power to act from unconscious sources, so does the present physical universe, as you know it rises from other dimensions. So does it have its source and derives its energy from more profound realities. Reality is far more diverse, far more prosperous, and unutterable than you can *presently* suppose or comprehend. (J. Roberts, 1972, pp. 237-238)

AN INNER AND OUTER
ORDER OF EVENTS

From a transpersonal perspective, there is an inner *and* outer order of events. The inner order of events is the source of the outer and forms the unseen framework for what William James (1936) called "the higher part of the universe" (p. 507). According to William James,

The unseen region in question is not merely ideal, for it produces effects in this world. When we commune with it, work is done upon our finite personality... But that which produces effects within another reality must be termed a reality itself, so I feel as if we have no intellectual excuse for calling the unseen or mystical world unreal... God is real since he produces real effects. (James, 1936, pp. 506-507)

In these terms, the apparition at Medjugorje is a reality in an inner order of events because it produces real effects in people's experience of themselves and their world. At that inner level, the apparition of the six youths of Medjugorje presents some very private information of significant importance to them from that nonphysical, inner order - intuitive and revelatory *transpersonal* knowledge far beyond the boundaries of their known selves that springs into physical existence to expand their conscious knowledge and experience.

However, as a reality in an inner order of events, it can only be expressed or manifested *symbolically* in the outer three-dimensional physical world of space and time. The excellent and significant creative material, the psychic content, becomes changed by the beliefs, symbols, ideas, and intents of the conscious mind of the six "visionaries" who must interpret the information they receive. The apparitions and messages the six youths receive thus represent the encounter of their personalities with the vast power of their psyche *and* with a multidimensional identity or consciousness, personified in dramatized form according to these six young people's ideas.

Like a round peg trying to fit a square hole, the resulting translation gives us events squeezed out of shape to some degree, as the six youths superimpose one kind of reality over another, interpreting one kind of information from the inner order *in terms of* the outer one, with all of its relatively conventional beliefs, symbols, ideas, and images, altering it to some extent. While instinctively sensing its multidimensional nature, the six Medjugorje youths' psyches deflect and distort the "Virgin Mary" personality to some degree and reflect it through their nature as it expresses itself through them. In this way, entirely legitimate and

Good psychological experiences of basically independent, alternate realities and actualities become clothed in the garb of minimal, conventional images and ideas of our time's religious and cultural beliefs.

A CRITICAL REALISM - ASPECT PSYCHOLOGY FRAMEWORK

This interpretation of the apparitions of Medjugorje is based on the Aspect Psychology of mystic and writer Jane Roberts (1975) and proceeds from what philosopher-theologian John Hick (1999) calls the "critical realist principle." Aspect Psychology posits the existence of "a basic creative undifferentiated reality -- an ever-present field of latent activity -- that springs into being as consciousness encounters it, and patterns it according to its perceptive focus" (Roberts, 1975, p. 180). Critical realism acknowledges the existence of external realities but only as they appear to us within the context of the culturally conditioned perceptual-conceptual- reflective system of the percipient. In the words of St. Thomas Aquinas: "Cognita sunt in cognoscente secundum modum cognoscenti" or "Things are known are in the knower according to the mode of the knower" (quoted in Hick, 1999, p. 43). Hick (1999) uses Julian of Norwich's visions of Christ to illustrate the difference between non-realist, naïve realist, and critical realist approaches to understanding religious phenomena.

Let's take as an example. . . .Julian of Norwich's visions of Christ and her hearing him speak of the limitless divine love. The non-realist interpretation is that the entire experience was a self-induced hallucination – not in any sense a revelation, not an expression of the 'impact' of the Transcendent upon her. The naïve realist interpretation

-- which was probably her understanding of her experiences – is that the living Christ was personally present to her, producing the visions that she saw and uttering in Middle English the words that she heard. But the critical realist interpretation, which I believe to be correct, is that she had become so open to the transcendent, within her and beyond her, that it flooded into her consciousness in the particular form provided by her Christian faith. ...Her experience was thus a genuine contact with the Transcendent, but clothed in her case in a Christian rather than a Hindu, Buddhist, Islamic, or another form.....In these and many other ways, the transcendent reality's impact upon us receives different 'faces' and voices as our different religious mentalities process it. Religious experience, then, occurs in many different forms, and the critical realist interpretation enables us to see how these may nevertheless be different authentic responses to the Real. But they may also not be. They may instead be human self-delusion. Or they may be a mixture of both, and so a critical stance about them is essential. (pp. 42-43)

Each of these interpretations can be applied to the apparitions of Medjugorje as well.

The transpersonal interpretation of the apparitions of Medjugorje proposed here also draws upon the theoretical framework that mystic and writer Jane Roberts (1975) termed Aspect Psychology - "a framework through which previously denied psychic elements of life could be viewed as proper, beneficial, and natural conditions of our consciousness" (p. v). According to this theory, the six youths of Medjugorje's apparitions represent messages from multidimensional aspects of ourselves to selves who are in space and time. Imprinted by their psychological field and sifted through the personalities of the percipients, the phenomenon - the appearance of the Blessed Mary - appears in line with the six youth's ideas of Christianity and personality *the phenomenon's reality might exist in different terms entirely.* Symbolization and personification are important psychologically. As Jung noted, the "Virgin Mary" personality is a symbol (or archetype) for other dimensions of our personality. Thus, the Virgin Mary apparition may represent a deep part of the structure of the psyche of the six youths *as well as* a definite personification of a multi-reality consciousness (or Virgin Mary entity).

TRUE AND NOT TRUE

In specific terms, the apparitions of Medjugorje are real and not accurate. As representations of unconscious knowledge, they are right; as representations of physical reality, they are false, in the same way, that a map is not the territory, the menu is not the meal, the sign is not the destination, and the written or spoken word is not the thought or feeling it intends to convey or express. Symbols are not to be taken literally or mistaken for the reality they represent. People encounter difficulty when they mistake the symbol for reality during their encounter with the inner order events. When we do mistake the symbolic appearance for the reality itself, we inevitably misunderstand its nature.

This is not to say that there is no reality behind the symbols. As Jung correctly understood, the world of imagination and so-called symbols and myths are in many ways more real or closer to the way reality is than what is often referred to as physical, material, "sensory-hard" facts or phenomenon we can see, hear, feel smell, and touch (Jung, 1960). Dreams, ideas, emotions, values, and other aspects of psychological life are as real and, in some instances, more real than the chair upon which we sit because of their effect upon our experience of ourselves and our world. Television characters of a favorite TV program, for example, may attain a level of reality that is more real, more tangible, and more substantial than the lives of the actual actors who portray those characters in the mind of its viewers. Imaginative constructs, such as Darwin's theory of evolution, Freud's speculation about the nature of personality, Existentialism's philosophy about the nature of existence, and science's "Big Bang" conjecture about the origin of the universe have structured generations of people's experience of themselves and their world. Nor is it sufficiently appreciated how waking experience is directed, cultures and civilizations are formed, and religious and political structures are maintained by using our imaginative abilities. In many ways, the world of the imagination is the closest we can presently come to the inside of so-called "facts" and the realities from which facts emerge (Brann, 1991).

Suppose it turns out that the BVM apparitions have not occurred in any place or at any time to the youths of Medjugorje, but because our species has created the BVM myth, the Medjugorje youth created the apparitions out of our need. Consider how the BVM apparitions and messages have enabled the percipients and all those faithful who endure the pilgrimage's hardships to Medjugorje to give to their religious feeling objectivity that it would not otherwise have. And how the apparitions and Marian Messages represent for believers a link to the vital reality behind a God concept (or whatever term you want to use) that represents our species' unconscious knowledge of some more significant Source, supreme reality, or "dynamic ground" out of which our existence constantly springs and in which we are always couched, connected and rooted (Washburn, 1995). This apparition which historically may not have occurred as the proponents say it occurred nevertheless has a reality. More than it would have had, had it occurred in so-called historical fact.

Jung recognized that humanity has always projected unassimilated portions of its psychological reality outward, personifying them, using at various times a variety of images that make up the pantheon of gods and goddesses, good spirits and bad (Jung, Von Franz, Henderson, Jacobi, & Jaffe, 1964). All these "forces" have had an essential part to play in our species' psychological evolution, as documented in the mythologies that have been handed down to us across the ages (Campbell, 1949). There are an essential dynamism and vitality to our God concepts that go beyond being simple intellectual containers for "religious sentiments" (All port, 1955/1969, p. 98). I believe our constructed concepts of God act as transpersonal symbols of intuitive insight and transmitters for impulses toward "higher" development stages that arise from deeper dimensions of our species' nature. God's various ideas that our species create are intuitive projections intended to give conscious direction to the area crucial as stimulators of development and evolution,go3). Seemingly outside of the self, our constructed images, symbols, and concepts of God not only reflect the State of our consciousness as it "is" and points toward its desired future state and is meant to lead development stage most generous areas of fulfillment (Assagioli, 1991; J. Roberts, 1981).

The apparitions of Medjugorje can be considered in a similar light. They stand for those sensed but unknown glimpses of our reality that we as a species are determined to explore. The apparitions of Medjugorje, in distorted form, reflect those greater actualities of an inner order of being. The problem is in making symbolic personifications literal (for has not science taught us that only "literal fact" is actual?) and never looking behind the symbolism of the communication, beyond the inner morality play, for the more significant meanings beneath.

Mirjana, one of the six visionaries of Medjugorje, was the first visionary to receive all the Ten Secrets. Our Lady has given her the responsibility to reveal the secrets to the world when it is time. Our Lady gave Mirjana a parchment with all the secrets written on them. It is made of a material not found on this earth. The following is an interview with Mirjana in June of 1988 during the Caritas Medjugorje Documentary filming called The Lasting Sign. Mirjana, at this time, was not married and living in Sarajevo with Her family. Mirjana was asked about the parchment given to her by Our Lady containing the Ten Secrets.

QUESTION:

"Would you tell us now about the parchment that relates to the secrets?
Mirjana: "On this parchment, I have ten secrets, with the dates and the places where they are going to take place. That parchment I should give to the priest of my choice. Ten days before the secret, I will give this paper to him. He will only be able to see the secret that is going to happen. He will only be able to see the first secret. He will pray and fast on bread and water. On the third day before the secret is divulged, he will make it public – that this and that will happen at this and this place. This should be convincing that Our Lady had been here – that She did not call us in vain to peace, to love, to conversion.

Q: *"Where is the parchment now?*

Me: *"In my room. When I got all the ten secrets, I was always afraid that I might forget
something. I was not sure about myself to remember all those dates. It gave me trouble all the
time. So one day, while I had the vision, Mary gave me that; we call it foil, that parchment. It
is neither a paper nor a tissue or fabric – just like an old pigment parchment. All ten secrets
are nicely written on it, so I keep that paper in the drawer with the rest of my papers. I
showed it to a cousin of mine, and she just saw a letter. She did not see any secrets; she just
saw it as a letter. And I showed it to, and I think it was my aunt. I showed it to her, and she
just saw individual poems. Nobody sees the same. Only me, only I can see the secrets, so there
is no danger – I don't have to hide it, to conceal it. I can keep it on the table because nobody
can read it, the secrets.*

Q: *"When you show it to other people, don't they notice that it is a particular texture or form
that it is not ordinary paper – even though they can't read anything on it?*

M: *They were all confused. One saw it was a song, and one saw it was a letter. They were
surprised. So I thought something was wrong with that, so I should not show it to anybody
else. It caused laughter, surprise. I just folded the paper and put it away in my drawer."* [1]

Our Lady told Mirjana to choose a priest that would be responsible for revealing the secrets.
Mirjana chose Fr. Petar Ljubicic. Fr. Ljubicic was interviewed by a Friend of Medjugorje for
Radio Wave in 2008. In a part of the interview, Fr. Petar was asked what he knew about the
parchment.

Q: *"Have you ever seen the parchment or held the parchment?*
Fr. Petar: *"Some people I know, they did tell me that they have seen it. I never did. Some of
her cousins saw it...And Our Lady then said to Mirjana, do not show this to anyone yet, until
the time of the revelation comes. Mirjana, during the war, was in Sarajevo. When she
returned, she forgot the parchment and left it in Sarajevo. A year or two ago, a soldier
brought it to her with all the belongings that she left behind during the war. She asked him,
'how did you know this parchment belongs to me.' He said, 'I had a feeling in my soul that I*

should bring this to you.' I don't know what is here, but this is what happens with this parchment. Again, something I would say is miraculous.

Q: "Wow, so this man did not know Mirjana?

Fr. Petar: "No, he just brought it to her house, and that is it. But he didn't know her in Sarajevo, and he didn't know that she was living in Sarajevo at the time."
Hidden Miracles of Medjugorje
Sometimes miracles happen right in front of us and still go unnoticed.
The *Stella Mar Films* team put together this **special report from Medjugorje** to highlight one aspect of Mirjana's apparitions that is sometimes overlooked—but is perhaps a **miracle** hidden in plain sight.

On the 18th of March, I had the honor of assisting Mirjana up the hill and kneeling beside her during the apparition—although I jokingly thanked her for helping *me* get up the hill.
For anyone skeptical about the apparitions, I wish they could have the chance to see and feel what I did. Their doubts would be wiped away in an instant. They would have no choice but to admit that they had witnessed a miracle—and although you can see it happen in our video, this miracle is often hidden in plain sight.
That's why I'm compelled to share my experience with you now...

Mirjana prefers to experience the apparitions at the Blue Cross, located at the base of Apparition Hill, but that has more to do with everyone else than with herself.
She suffers from a knee and back condition which causes her severe pain when she climbs up the steep slope to reach the Blue Cross. Despite the pain, however, she is always determined to experience the apparition among the thousands of people who gather on the hill—unless the weather is too severe.

"How can I be with Blessed Mary alone at home when I look out and see all the pilgrims who come to Medjugorje seeking her?" she says.
Everyone in Medjugorje expected the March 18th apparition to happen in Mirjana's home. The local weather forecast had been calling for heavy rain, which would have made the slippery rocks too dangerous to climb.
Surprisingly, however, the weather was sunny and unseasonably warm in the hours leading up

to 2 p.m., the approximate time at which Mirjana expected Our Lady to appear to her.

At around 1:30 p.m., Mirjana left her home and made her way through the crowd of pilgrims, eventually coming to the base of Apparition Hill. She had asked me to come with her—and of course, I didn't hesitate.

My co-filmmaker, Cimela Kidonakis, was already at the Blue Cross with her camera, ready to film the apparition, along with our group of pilgrims who had traveled with us from the USA. Our guide, Miki Musa, was also there with his notebook ready to translate the message, and the fantastic people from *Foto Dani*—the local video and photo team that documents all that happens in Medjugorje—were busy capturing the moment.

I walked by Mirjana's side so she could lean on me whenever it got complicated. Like always, people were shouting her name, but on this particular day, they also wished her a happy birthday in many different languages. "Buon compleanno!" "Sretan rodendan!" "Feliz cumpleanos!"

The pain intensified in her knees and back as she ascended the steep, rocky path, getting worse with each step, and yet she still paused to smile at the eager pilgrims as she went. I'm always amazed at Mirjana's love for the pilgrims. She stopped to greet some of them on her way, especially the sick and disabled.

Mirjana spoke at a Marian Conference in Chicago in 1998. She was asked the following question about the Lasting Sign:

Question: "Has Our Lady given any indication that She will leave a sign or miracle at Medjugorje as She did at Fatima?

Mirjana: "Yes, Our Lady will leave a sign at the Hill of Apparitions, and everybody will see that she was truly present there and that it's something from God. And the sign will be something that it will be clear that human hands could not have created when you see it. But you won't see it from America, and you'll have to come there to see it. Pilgrims from the United States often ask me if we will be able to see it from home or will we have to go there to see it."

In a series of other interviews, the visionaries were asked questions about the Lasting Sign. The following is their responses:

Question: "Mirjana, what, if anything, are you permitted to tell us about the Ten Secrets?
Mirjana: "The first two secrets come as warnings for the whole world and as proof that the Blessed Mother is here in Medjugorje.
Question: "And the third secret?
Mirjana: "The third secret will be a visible sign at Medjugorje – permanent, indestructible, and beautiful." 5

Marija:

Question: "For clarification purposes, the great sign for all non-believers, will it take place on Apparition Mountain behind us or where will it take place?
Marija: "Our Lady told us that She would leave the sign on the Hill of the Apparitions.
Question: "Is there anything you can tell us about the sign the Blessed Mother has promised to leave us?
Marija: "It will be a visible sign for all the unbelievers to see. But, for those that already believe, they do not need a sign." 6
Question: "You and the other visionaries have indicated that there will be advanced signs [signs preceding the great sign] in many places in the world to warn the world. When will these advanced signs begin?
Marija: "There are signs in many places in the world now. Many people see luminary signs. Many experienced personal healings, both physical and spiritual, and also psychological. Many have private signs. People have come here from all over the world. Often they have or have had great signs in their lives.

Question: "Will all people on earth believe in God, in the Blessed Mother, when the permanent sign occurs?

Marija: "The Blessed Mother has said that those who are still alive when the permanent sign comes will witness many conversions among the people because of the sign, but She also says blessed are those who do not see but who believe.

Question: "Mirjana told me that there will still be some unbelievers even when the permanent sign comes.

Marija: "The Blessed Mother has said there will always be Judases.

Question: "Vicka told me that there is great urgency in the Blessed Mother's call to immediate conversion. She said that those who only marginally believe, who choose to wait for the great sign to believe, it would be too late. Do you know why it will be too late for them?

Marija: "This is a time of great grace and mercy. Now is the time to listen to these messages and to change our lives. Those who do will never be able to thank God enough." 7

Jakov:

Question: "Do you know when the permanent sign is coming, Jakov?

Jakov: "Yes. When the permanent sign comes, people will come here from all over the world in even larger numbers. Many more will believe.

Question: "Will all people believe because of the permanent sign, Jakov?

Jakov: "The Blessed Mother said that there will still be some who will not believe even after the permanent sign comes.

Question: "Do you know what the permanent sign is, Jakov?

Jakov: "Yes.

Question: "Can you tell us anything about it?

Jakov: "It will be something that has never been on the earth before.

Question: "Jakov, why will some still not believe?

Jakov: "They will not put themselves in a position to be converted." 8

REFERENCES

All port, G. W. (1955/1969). *Becoming.* New Haven, CT: Yale University Press. (Original work published 1955).

Apparitions of Jesus and Mary (2004, January 7).

Retrieved May 28, 2008,

Armstrong, K. (1993). *A history of God.* New York: Ballantine Books. Assagioli, R. (1991). *Transpersonal development.* England: Crucible.

Brann, E. T. H. (1991). *The world of imagination.* Lanham, MD: Rowman & Littlefield.

Campbell, J. (1949). *Hero with a thousand faces.* New York: The World Publishing Company.

Davies, M. (2004). *Medjugorje after twenty-one years: The definitive history.*

Retrieved May 24, 2008.

Dowling, S. J. (1984). Lourdes cures and their medical assessment. *Journal of the Royal Society of Medicine, 77,* 634-638.

First Days (2006, May 26). Retrieved May 24, 2008.

Foley, D. (2002). *Marian apparitions, the Bible, and the modern world.* Herefordshire, England: Grace Wing Press.

Franken, R. (1999). *A journey to Medjugorje.* Netherlands: Van Spijk.

Gramaglia, P. A. (1987). L'Equivoco di Medjugorje: Apparizioni Mariane o Fenameni di Medianita? Toronto, Canada: Claudiana.

Grof, S. (1985). *Beyond the brain.* Albany, NY: State University of New York Press.

Hastings, A. (1991). *With tongues of men and angels.* Fort Worth, TX: Holt.

Hick, J. (1999). *The fifth dimension.* Oxford: Oneworld.

James, W. (1902/1936). *The varieties of religious experiences.* New York: Modern Library. (Original work published in 1902)

Jones, E. M. (1994). *Medjugorje: The untold story.* South Bend, IN Fidelity Press.

Jung, C. G. (1960). *The structure and dynamics of the psyche. Vol. 8.* In H. Read, M. Fordham, and G. Adler (Eds.), *The collected works of C. G. Jung.* New York: Pantheon.

Jung, C. G., Von Franz, M-L., Henderson, J. L., Jacob, J., & Jaffe, A. (Eds.). (1964). *Man and his symbols.* Garden City, NY: Doubleday.

Klimo, J. (1987). *Channeling.* Los Angeles: Tarcher.

Laurentin, R. ((1987). *The apparitions at Medjugorje prolonged.* Milford, OH: The Riehle Foundation.

Myers, F. W. H. (1976). *The subliminal consciousness.* New York; Arno Press. (Reprint of articles initially published in 1889-95, in vols. 5, 6, 8, 9, and 11 of Proceedings of the Society for Psychical Research)

Roberts, J. (1970). *The Seth Material.* Englewood Cliffs, NJ: Prentice-Hall Roberts, J. (1972). *Seth speaks.* Englewood Cliffs, Prentice-Hall.

Roberts, J. (1975). *Adventures in consciousness.* Englewood Cliffs, NJ: Prentice-Hall Roberts, J. (1981). *The God of Jane.* Englewood Cliffs, NJ: Prentice-Hall.

Roberts, T. (2001). *Psychoactive sacramentals.*San Francisco: Council on Spiritual Practices. Sivric, I. (1989). *The hidden side of Medjugorje.* Quebec, Canada: Psilog.

Washburn, M. (1995). *The ego and the dynamic ground.* Albany, NY: State University of New York Press.